## For J. H.

Thanks to Dr. Sean Hearne,
Sandia National Laboratories, Albuquerque, New Mexico,
for his advice and suggestions.

G. P. PUTNAM'S SONS
A division of Penguin Young Readers Group. Published by The Penguin Group.
Penguin Group (USA) Inc., 375 Hudson Street, New York, NY 10014, U.S.A.

Penguin Group (Canada), 90 Eglinton Avenue East, Suite 700, Toronto, Ontario, Canada M4P 2Y3 (a division of Pearson Penguin Canada Inc.). Penguin Books Ltd, 80 Strand, London WC2R 0RL, England. Penguin Ireland, 25 St. Stephen's Green, Dublin 2, Ireland (a division of Penguin Books Ltd.). Penguin Group (Australia), 250 Camberwell Road, Camberwell, Victoria 3124, Australia (a division of Pearson Australia Group Pty Ltd). Penguin Books India Pvt Ltd, 11 Community Centre, Panchsheel Park, New Delhi - 110 017, India. Penguin Group (NZ), Cnr Airborne and Rosedale Roads, Albany, Auckland 1310, New Zealand (a division of Pearson New Zealand Ltd). Penguin Books (South Africa) (Pty) Ltd, 24 Sturdee Avenue, Rosebank, Johannesburg 2196, South Africa. Penguin Books Ltd, Registered Offices: 80 Strand, London WC2R 0RL, England.

Published simultaneously in Canada. Manufactured in China by South China Printing Co. Ltd. Design by Gunta Alexander. Text set in Bawdy Bold.
The art was done in watercolors and gouache. Airbrush backgrounds by Joseph Hearne.

Library of Congress Cataloging-in-Publication Data
Brett, Jan, 1949–  Hedgie blasts off! / Jan Brett.  p. cm.  Summary: When the spectacular, sparkling explosions at a popular tourist sight slow down, Hedgie the hedgehog is the only one capable of flying to tiny planet Mikkop to see what is wrong. [1. Astronauts—Fiction. 2. Janitors—Fiction. 3. Hedgehogs—Fiction. 4. Science fiction.]  I. Title.  PZ7.B75225Big 2006  [E]—dc22  2005032654  ISBN 0-399-24621-5

1 3 5 7 9 10 8 6 4 2

First Impression

**M**y name is Hedgie and I want to be an astronaut.

I work at Star Lab on the cleanup crew. I've never flown on a spaceship, but I take care of the Zeppadoppler rocket for the Professor, the smartest scientist on Earth. He's in charge of Outer Space.

Today when I got to work, the Professor looked worried.

"Hedgie, we have a problem," he said. "Big Sparkler is only sending up weak bursts of sparkles. If it stops altogether, there will be no more Big Sparkler and no more flowers."

Big Sparkler is on the tiny planet of Mikkop. Alien tourists love to fly over it to watch it erupt and to take pictures of the strange flowers that depend on the sparkles for food.

"This is an emergency, Hedgie. Call the scientists to the lab."

The scientists came in and the Professor explained the problem.

"Big Sparkler is failing," he told them. "We need to go to Mikkop and find out what's wrong. I'd fly there in the Zeppadoppler, but it is too big to land on tiny Mikkop. We need to build a Rescue Robot and a small rocket to go there."

The scientists looked at the drawings on the blackboard and went to work. I tried to help.

Soon everything was ready for the launch. Reporters came to hear about the mission.

The Professor explained. "Big Sparkler isn't working properly," he said. "First let me show you how it is supposed to work."

He put a cork in a bottle of fizzy water. "Pretend this is Big Sparkler." He shook and shook the bottle until the cork flew out and water soaked the reporters.

"But now Big Sparkler is sending up fewer and fewer sparkles. We think it may stop altogether!" the Professor said.

"How can you find out what is going on?" a reporter asked.

"Meet Rescue Robot!" the Professor answered. He threw open the hatch to the rocket. The pilot's seat was empty.

We looked all around the lab. No robot. Then I opened the door to the cleanup crew closet. There he was, in sleeper mode, spikes jammed fast. Rescue Robot had probed too soon, gotten stuck, and crashed.

The reporters looked at the Professor. The Professor looked at me and at Rescue Robot. Then he whispered in my ear.

"Hedgie, you are the only one who will fit into the rocket. How would you like to go to Outer Space?"

I nodded my head YES!

The Professor turned to the reporters. "A little change of plans," he told them. "Meet Rescue Hedgie. No programming necessary!"

The Professor looked at me. "Come back and tell us what you find, Hedgie, and we will fix the problem."

**ZOOM!**

The tiny planet Mikkop got larger
and larger before my eyes.

The engines roared as the rocket settled onto Mikkop's surface.
I climbed out of the hatch. Big Sparkler's crater was in front of me.
The flowers circling it had turned into little gray puffballs.

Suddenly I was startled by a low flying saucer. It buzzed down
just as Big Sparkler struggled to erupt. A thin stream of glittery
sparkles sifted through the air and dusted the passing ship.
The tourists inside shrieked and threw things out of their
portholes and into the crater.

## clink, clank, clunk!

More squeals! Then I saw what was falling into the crater. Coins!

I walked over and looked down. So that's what was wrong. Too many coins from all over the galaxy were filling up Big Sparkler. It needed to be cleaned out.

I wanted to fix Big Sparkler for the Professor before going home. But how could I drag all those years of coins out of the crater? It was impossible for one small hedgehog.

Then I remembered the bottle of fizzy water and the cork. What if I became the cork for Big Sparkler! One small hedgehog might just be perfect for the job.

I took a big jump before I was too scared.

I landed in the opening and puffed up
my prickles to stop it up completely. I told myself,
"Just hold fast with every prickle."

I felt Big Sparkler pushing against me. The more it pushed,
the tighter I held on. Hold fast! Hold fast! Hold fast!

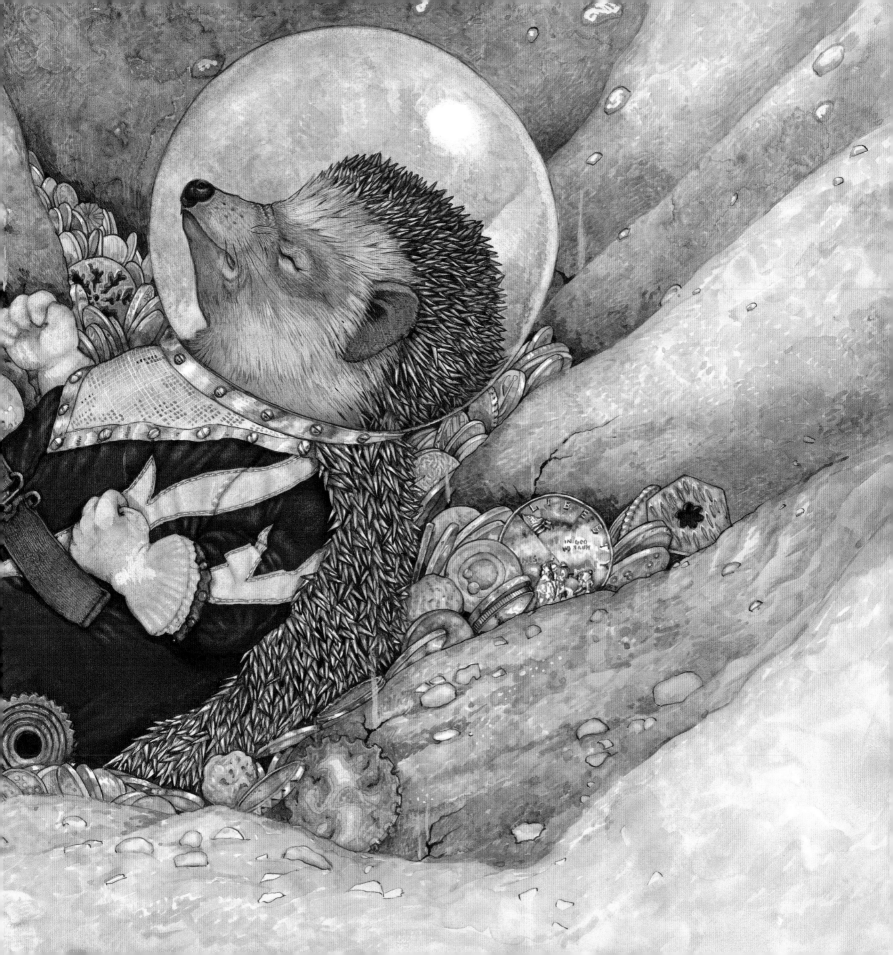

Big Sparkler
erupted with
a tremendous roar.
I flew up . . .

. . . and landed in a soft pile of sparkles. Giant flowers came alive right before my eyes.

I raced back to the rocket and took off for home. I was making a victory orbit around Mikkop when I saw the alien tourists. They were squealing with joy. Instead of throwing good-luck coins into Big Sparkler, they were trying to catch them flying through space. I hope it takes years for them to collect all those coins!

Back at Star Lab, I was in for another surprise. I stood beside the Professor as he said a few words to the reporters.

"Please meet our first hedgehog astronaut. The scientists at Star Lab proudly present Hedgie with the Official Astronaut Star for his courage and cool thinking."

I was an astronaut!

The Professor went on, "Star Lab is grateful to everyone who worked to save Mikkop and Big Sparkler—from Astronaut First Class Hedgie to our new high-tech cleanup crew."

"Three cheers for Hedgie! Hurray!"